# DETENTION

"Even those you trust most can let
you down; never trust anyone."

Shaya Dadmehr

# CONTENTS

# CHAPTER 1: ARE MY TEACHERS DEMONS?

**B**radford is who you would consider a profoundly smart, nerdy, and slightly socially awkward kid. Although he's only 14-years-old, he's a junior in high school because he skipped three grades. He has blue eyes, slightly tilted glasses, messy stringy red hair, and freckles on his cheeks. He is the biggest teacher's pet on earth, which means he has very few friends—one to be exact. He's highly analytical and a huge techie. Every day, he walks down the same hall, wearing the same glasses and pinstripe suit, and executes the same monotonous acts, i.e., acing every test. (Monotonous is a word that means repetitive and boring.)

However, one day, this all changed. Just as he was walking down the hall as he usually did to get to his 4th period AP Physics class, he was approached by two awkward kids, maybe even slightly weirder than him. They seemed to be panicked. Bradford tried to inch away from them, but they kept hovering closer and closer. They may have been new to the school or may have been in the remedial classes, which were designed for kids with learning deficiencies. Bradford was always in the accelerated classes in every subject, and he only knew a few faces, the one face he could never forget was his friend Andy's face.

Andy was a talkative friend, for a nerd. He too had red hair like Bradford, and they both stood about five feet five inches tall. Unlike Bradford, Andy had buck teeth, the darkest of brown eyes, perfectly groomed curly hair, and no freckles or glasses. They were in all the same classes except for AP Spanish, and they were always lab partners. They never argued or fought because they spent most of their time reading. Bradford really enjoyed reading as it opened his imagination to new things, like flying dragons, prancing ponies, and demented demon novels, which were truly a life-changing experience for him. Speaking of demented demon novels, this very moment made Bradford feel like he was in one as the two boys rushed him and shoved him inside the bathroom.

Bradford's head was flooding with panic. Maybe they were just bullies. They couldn't be much worse than the jocks. They still had that distressed aura circling around them as if they were panicked. This was the thing that was really making Bradford uneasy. Once in the bathroom, there was a long awkward silence, which gave Bradford time to study their features. Both looked to be 17 years old, and both juniors like him but three years older than him. He studied the boy across from him. He had long blond locks with sea blue eyes and seemed to be wondering about something disturbing. The other boy had short black hair and murky green eyes.

"Hello, can I help you?" asked Bradford.

The one with blond hair said, "We need your help. If you haven't noticed, for the past few weeks, kids have disappeared from school, and we want to find out why."

For a split second, Bradford thought this must be a hoax. Although he had noticed the diminishing school population, he had attributed the decrease to kids dropping out. He voiced his thoughts, and the boys gazed at him in disbelief.

"You haven't been there, have you?" spat the boy with black hair.

"Been where? When?" Bradford looked at the boys, perplexed.

He then brushed off his thoughts and looked at his Fitbit edition nine Goku dragon watch. He had two minutes to get to class, and he had never been tardy to any class with the exception of P.E. Bradford said, "I have to go," and thundered out the door in a jog and then a complete sprint, but he wasn't sprinting to get to class. He was sprinting to get away from those creeps. While running, many thoughts raced in his head. What were those kids talking about—been where?

He arrived at class in the nick of time and took his seat at the front of the room, right across from the teacher, so he could voice all his boring opinions, hypotheses, and explanations, causing most kids to doze off without taking notes.

Today, though, there was something wrong. Bradford didn't raise his hand for every question. He only raised his hand 36 out of the 42 possible times. Only people who knew Bradford well could tell something was wrong.

During lunch, Andy approached Bradford and asked, "Is something the matter?"

Bradford sharply replied, "No!" and walked away.

He needed some alone time to process what those two boys in the bathroom were talking about. He then decided that after school he would go back to that bathroom and see if those crazed kids were still lurking around.

As that uncanny, or in other words, mysterious or strange, day passed, Bradford nudged the negative thoughts out of his head and went to his classes. Today seemed like a normal day, but something was in the air. Bradford could tell it wasn't truly like an ordinary day of learning, analyzing, and getting bullied. There was something eerie about today. Throughout the day, Bradford heard some odd and bothersome noises that resembled faint cries followed by gritty laughter.

As the dismissal bell rang, Bradford ran by the bathroom to see if the two crazy kids were still lurking around, but there was no sign of them. However, Bradford still heard some faint screaming noises, so he mustered up all his courage and sprinted and barged into the bathroom.

"Is there anyone th-th-there?" Bradford stuttered. "If you're there, I'm, I'm... going to kill you with my... very bulky and... muscular arms!" (He was bluffing.).

Suddenly, two boys burst out of a stall and yanked him in. This stall was like the one in Dr. Who. It appears small on the outside and huge on the inside.

It was those same creepy kids again! Bradford wasn't sure if he was relieved or terrified. After all, he wanted to see those kids again.

"We meet again," snarled the boy with black hair.

"Chill man. You sound like you're going to murder him. How about we calmly introduce ourselves," The boy with blond hair soothingly announced.

"Yeah, whatever...anyways, I'm Spike," said the black hair kid. "This is my friend, Maverick, and this is Maverick's sister, Miranda."

Miranda's long blonde locks bounced up and down as she inched closer, and her crystal blue eyes glistened like fireworks. She was truly breathtaking.

"Nice to meet you." Maverick extended his arm, and Bradford gladly shook his hand. Since they weren't about to murder him, it was a gigantic relief.

Miranda, who looked like a 15-year-old freshman, shook Bradford's hand, too. He knew he liked her, but there was no time to think or daydream about his crush. Bradford had to find out why these kids had basically abducted him. As Bradford folded his arms and raised his eyebrows, Spike proceeded.

"We sought you out because we need to get to the bottom of why and how all these kids have disappeared over the past few weeks and why the outside courtyard is nearly deserted," Spike informed Bradford.

*So, the outside courtyard is where they were referring to earlier.* It's true. Bradford rarely visited the outside courtyard. Nerds like him were not welcomed there, and other than being the laughingstock and/or the butt of a joke for the jocks' entertainment, there was nothing for Bradford in the courtyard.

"Well, we have a sneaking suspicion that the kids who disappeared have something to do with the teachers and administration who have been absent and/or acting strangely," Spike stated.

Spike was one of those kids who acted like he was a know-it-all and a divine ruler, who didn't have time for anyone else's thoughts or opinions other than his own. Bradford had noticed that substitute teachers were covering some of his classes and that some of his teachers were acting a bit peculiar, so he couldn't completely disregard Spike's claims. Bradford just attributed his teachers' absence and shift in behavior to his teachers being sick or having personal matters to take care of, not to them abducting and torturing kids and working for a supernatural evil force.

Bradford told himself this was preposterous, but he played along with the idea. After all, he could potentially make new friends. (Preposterous is a word that means absolutely crazy and contrary to reason or common sense; just the word preposterous sounds utterly absurd itself.)

"Anyways we're starting a secret club to investigate this conspiracy theory of the teachers working for the greater evil. We thought you would be resourceful because you know most of the teachers well, you're always the teacher's pet, and you're the smartest kid in the school," Maverick stated.

Although he was making a simple decision, Bradford was thinking hard, weighing the pros and cons, and contemplating his next move. Did he want to be the nerd he was and remain the teacher's pet, or did he join this club and possibly get expelled for this one pretty girl and her stupid friend and brother's dull-witted conspiracy? The moment he uttered his decision, he regretted it.

"Sure, I'd happily join your club. Are there other members?" Bradford inquired.

"No, this is a top secret and highly private club; we don't want too many members," Miranda explained with an intense look that seared right through Bradford's heart.

"Like Miranda stated, if a giant club forms called **'Foil the Demon Teachers Villainous Scheme,'** the teachers would totally impede our plans and throw us in their petrifying dungeon or whatever they do with these poor unsuspecting kids," snapped Spike.

*Yeah, like no one knew that*, Bradford thought. He was truly starting to dislike and resent Spike. The way he talked to Bradford was extremely derogatory and terribly overbearing.

"Anyway, Bradford, we're meeting in front of the school at 4:15 a.m. sharp tomorrow morning to investigate. Will you join us?" Maverick asked.

Bradford was about to answer, but by a loud crashing noise, probably another fight, caught him off guard. He flinched and resumed what he was about to say. "Sure, I can meet you at school at 4:15 a.m., tomorrow morning."

As Bradford exited the stall, Miranda and Maverick waved bye while Spike just glared at him with curled lips.

Bradford scurried out of the bathroom, silently chuckling. This was Ridiculous with a capital "R"! Who could have possibly thought of a theory so outlandish?

While walking farther away from the bathroom, the nonsensical theory started to make more sense. Dang, those kids were even weirder than he initially thought, but strangely enough he also felt a beatific, in other words, happy, sensation surge throughout his entire body. Bradford only had one true friend and to possibly have more friends was exhilarating. Having new friends for Bradford was like having a surprise birthday party or skydiving out of a plane 10,000 feet above ground. It was the feeling of immense happiness that couldn't get any better, but yet extremely terrifying as if it could be the most life-threatening predicament that you could ever put yourself in, which Bradford was yet to discover.

Bradford was thinking of all that transpired, like joining the club, students disappearing, a deserted outdoor courtyard, and the so-called "demon teachers." He reassured himself that it was all a ruse, but he knew that if he didn't join the club, he wouldn't be able to see Miranda again, and that was an impossible scenario to think of for him. It would also be nice to be a superhero and save his fellow students. Maybe he would even become popular and stop getting bullied at school. The more Bradford thought about the conspiracy theory, the more he was inclined to think this conspiracy may be true.

Bradford strolled into his house, plopped himself on his bed, and started to do his homework. He usually enjoyed homework, but today, he didn't feel like doing it which bothered him. He thought it was the stupid conspiracy theory that those kids put in his head, which was preventing him from concentrating on his homework.

He tried to shrug it off and get back to his homework, but it was easier said than done. After completing his challenging homework, Bradford thought more and more about this conspiracy theory. He was thinking of every minute detail that may debunk the notion that his teachers were demons. He kept murmuring to himself, "This isn't true. This isn't true." Bradford just couldn't drop the idea.

The more he thought about it, the more puzzle pieces he merged, such as why did the class clown, Johnny, suddenly and allegedly move to a different country? Bradford never liked Johnny, but he knew he would have never wanted him to get eaten by a demon monster or something along those lines. And how that one parent was frantically complaining that her kid didn't come home, and how the school office staff awkwardly told the lady to follow him into a private office.

He cupped his face in his hands and muttered, "Have I been admiring and looking up to demon teachers?" But Bradford just repeated again and again, "This isn't true. This isn't true." Nevertheless, he needed an explanation. He always enjoyed detective books and prided himself on solving the plot before he finished reading the book. At the moment, he felt as if he was a detective in a book titled, ***Are My Teachers Demons?*** He laughed at himself, but he knew this could be very serious if proven true. He decided he would take the conspiracy theory seriously and start investigating tomorrow morning when he met up with Miranda, Maverick, and Spike.

Bradford didn't have much of an appetite. Since his mom was away on a business trip, he didn't feel like making himself anything to eat, so he swiftly brushed his teeth, put on his pjs, and jumped into bed. He consoled himself not to worry and that all his questions would be answered tomorrow. Bradford fell asleep, unaware of the trouble that laid ahead of him.

# CHAPTER 2: I DIDN'T KNOW YOU COULD ORDER SQUIRRELS

Bradford woke up to a startling sound. Worry rapidly flushed over him. Were the evil demon teachers on the attack? No! That couldn't be. How would the teachers know where he lived? The sound was reverberating from the attic. Oh, no, Bradford had always read in books that whenever someone went into the attic, they died a horrific death. He crept up into the attic solicitously, meaning anxiously, with his flashlight beaming in his quivering hand.

The banging intensified. CLANG! CLANG! But when Bradford peered in, he saw nothing but a single blank sheet of paper. What could it mean or say? He stealthily walked up to the sketchy piece of paper and could hear his heart pounding rapidly. THUMP. THUMP. THUMP. THUMP. He anxiously flipped the paper over; suspense consuming him. As he scrutinized the piece of paper with intense interest, it appeared to be an ordinary sheet of paper. Bradford carefully attempted to read the message as to not miss a word, but before he began to read, the paper disintegrated into nothing but atoms.

He shivered and stuttered, "Is anyone th-th-there?"

It was chilly in his attic, so it was hard not to shiver, but Bradford being Bradford ignored his instincts and shouted, "Get out of here right now, before you die!" He mustered up all his courage, walked across the attic, and witnessed something astonishing, standing adjacent to him. It was a tall, black, lean figure with two radiant evil eyes and blood dripping from his fangs. He was beaming straight at Bradford with a villainous, devilish smile. Bradford wanted to yelp, but before he could, he noticed something that almost made him jump out of his socks, a name tag that read: "Mr. Abram" on this mysterious man's trench coat. At closer inspection, something was familiar about this man's figure.

"M-m-m-m-my AP Calculus teacher!" Bradford exclaimed.

He looked away for a split second, and when he glanced back, Mr. Abram had vanished. However, the piece of paper reappeared, and Bradford could now read the message. It read, "We're coming for you because you have what we need."

Bradford dropped the paper on the floor and ran out hastily bolting the attic door. He sprinted back down the hallway to his bedroom, pulled the covers over his head, and started counting sheep, but all he could see was Mr. Abram devouring the sheep, their blood splattering everywhere. How he wished his mom was home and not on a business trip! He was all alone and had no one to run to. Finally, after what seemed to be an eternity, Bradford passed out from pure exhaustion.

After a couple of hours of sleep, Bradford woke up three hours past midnight and raced to the attic to retrieve the note, written by Mr. Abram, as proof, but unfortunately, the note had vanished into thin air. He tried to shake off his imagination running wild. He skipped breakfast since he still had no appetite and mustered enough courage to go to school at 4 a.m. Still in his pajamas, he waited and waited until the gang showed up at 4:15 a.m. sharp. As soon as he spotted them, he darted over and told them about everything that had transpired the previous night with Mr. Abram. They nodded their heads as if they weren't surprised one bit.

Maverick said, "I'm glad that you believe us now. Let's get started and get to the bottom of this."

Miranda interjected, "Where is the only place in the entire school that students aren't allowed to enter?"

"The teacher's lounge!" Maverick responded.

"Maybe if we can find a way into the teacher's lounge, we can catch the teachers red-handed planning their evil plan?" Bradford said.

"But what if we get caught?" asked Spike.

"What's the worst that could happen? We could get detention, and that's it, right?" questioned Maverick.

"You're forgetting that they probably have

children in the vending machine and that detention is probably where these kids are disappearing," said Miranda.

Bradford had never received detention before, and he couldn't bear the thought of being detained. He then thought of Mr. Abram in his attic, and he couldn't help but shiver.

Bradford told himself, *this probably isn't true. This probably isn't true.*

He tried to convince himself that he had had a bad dream, that the whole Mr. Abram incident last night was just a nightmare, but deep down he knew last night was no nightmare.

School started at 8 a.m., and Bradford didn't expect anyone to be at school, but to his surprise he heard a loud and excruciating sound, like claws scratching against a chalkboard; Bradford hated that sound. Those horrible scratching noises made his knees buckle and his head throb, but instead of ignoring it, his gut told him to go towards it. He told the gang to stay behind while he checked out what was going on.

As he approached, the noise got louder, and he heard a conversation. He tried to listen as closely as possible without getting caught. The people conversing sounded like his teachers, but what were his teachers doing at school at 4:20 a.m.? Since he still couldn't make out what they were saying, Bradford crept even closer until he could kneel beside the open door and press his ear against the crack of the door.

"You are such a dunce," said a voice.

"Okay, just because I wanted to give a kid a little scare doesn't mean I'm a dunce," a second voice retorted.

"Anyway, who was this you scared?" a third voice hissed with annoyance.

Bradford realized that the person who spoke second was Mr. Abram, confirming that he didn't have a nightmare. Bradford was relieved about one thing. Mr. Abram didn't reveal Bradford's identity and referenced Bradford as "a kid". Shivers surged up his spine, and the freezing air seemed to get colder. Bradford didn't know how to process this. He felt an eerie sensation that he was being watched. He turned around and saw an image swiftly move behind him. Bradford was about to shout out to his friends and warn them, but then he remembered the teachers. He was about to signal to his friends that there was someone else lurking when the image appeared from the shadows.

The creeper was only Andy. What was Andy doing here so early in the morning? Bradford was about to walk back to his friends, but he noticed the teachers had stopped conversing.

*Oh no!* Bradford thought.

Whenever Bradford was bullied, he always told a teacher, but what happened if in this case, the bullies were the teachers? Would he tell the bullies? Since his mom was out of town, Bradford had no one to turn to other than his friends, who were in the same predicament as him.

"I smell children, the smell of disgusting kids who pick their noses, don't take showers, and sit on the couch playing video games all day," said a voice from inside the room.

This gave Bradford the chills, and as he looked back at his friends, they had vanished. Had they abandoned him to fend off these teachers who were about to thirst on his blood like a pack of hungry wolves? He noticed a pair of eyes in the bush, then another set, then one more set and one more. They must have been his friends. He didn't know what to do. Should he hide or run to his friends and give up their hiding spot and cause all of them to be killed? Bradford being Bradford went with the most logical option. He ran straight towards his friends.

(**Don't** is a commonly used word. You may say **don't** if someone was about to stick their hand in a beehive. If your mom says, "**Don't** do that," it means that she wants you to be safe by making sure you **don't** do something dangerous, for example, trying to get a cookie from the cookie jar with a stick while your cat with a cowboy hat is sitting on top of the jar, having a dance battle with the rat inside the cookie jar, is a **don't** because it will end up terribly for everyone. In this case, for Bradford, **don't** means **don't** run back to your friends with a pack of demons about to slaughter you when you're slow and unathletic and when you could have just as well hidden behind the door.)

Bradford heard a demon's low hiss

"I smell fear!" said a voice, sounding very

much like Mrs. Bloomer, his AP Physics teacher.

"And I hear a child running!" exclaimed a voice, oddly sounding like Ms. Mowie, his AP History teacher.

"And I'm feeling really hungry!" a voice said, which sounded exactly like Coach Rogers.

Bradford jumped in the bush the exact second that the demons busted through the doorway of the classroom where they had been discussing their retched plans, looking as bloodthirsty as could be.

"Come out, come out wherever you are." The teachers all started to laugh.

Bradford saw all his teachers—Mr. Abram, Mrs. Bloomer, Ms. Mowie, Coach Rogers, Ms. Maegan, his AP English teacher, and Mrs. Ramirez, his AP Spanish teacher. Bradford tried not to scream like a five-year-old girl. He looked next to him expecting to see his friends, but that was not what he saw.

He stared straight into the faces of four squirrels looking right back at him, and he almost fainted. The squirrels seemed more scared than Bradford as they ran out of the bushes. The teachers looked straight at the bush, formed an arch, and closed in on Bradford.

"Look at who we have here," Mr. Abram announced triumphantly.

But as he spread the hedges, he saw nothing.

"There's nothing here. It must've just been those squirrels," Mr. Abram said gloomily.

"I'm still hungry!" Coach Rogers ranted.

"Who wants to have squirrel kebab instead?" Mrs. Ramirez asked.

"Me!" All the teachers answered in unison as they marched away in search of squirrels to shish kebab.

Bradford was trying so hard not to pee his pants, hiding underneath a loose floorboard that was oddly located beneath the bushes. He heard the marching of the teachers as they were intensely cheering as if they were in a parade and still couldn't process what was happening.

Bradford's thoughts looked somewhat like this. *Teachers equal demons. Teachers eat squirrels. Teachers eat kids. Friends ran away from me. I'm claustrophobic and not getting enough oxygen, and I should probably get out from under this floorboard and try to find my friends or move to Afghanistan. The Afghanistan idea seems most appealing.*

Bradford wanted to stay under that floorboard forever, knowing the teachers were too stupid to find him under there. Yet he knew that wasn't realistic.

He was about to get out from underneath the floorboard when the sound of footsteps inched closer.

"Those squirrels are too quick for us," said Mrs. Ramirez.

"Can't we just order some squirrels on Door-Dash?" asked Coach Rogers.

"No, only Uber Eats delivers squirrels," Mr. Abram retorted.

Bradford wanted to laugh because just yesterday he had admired and looked up to these teachers, but now he realized how stupid these teachers were to think that Uber Eats delivered squirrels. However, worse than how stupid they were was the crazy realization that the teachers he so admired were DEMONS!

As you read this, you're probably reading with no emotions but imagine being in Bradford's shoes. Well, they were really sweaty, just kidding, but imagine how Bradford felt at this moment if your idols tried to eat you as an early-morning snack. At least, having someone as a main course is more respectable, don't you think?

Bradford heard the clamoring of his teachers' shoes right above him as they bickered about what to eat. Bradford held his breath, but he only had one thing on his mind and that was to locate his friends. As he exhaled, he heard the shuffling of his teachers' footsteps becoming more distant, followed by the screeching of a door hinge opening and then shutting with no more noise within earshot.

Bradford thought, *It's now or never*. He stealthily got out from underneath the floorboard and took a quick glance to make sure the teachers weren't setting a trap, and silently he dashed out of the bushes and turned the corner.

# CHAPTER 3: IS EVERYONE A DEMON?

Bradford kept running. He didn't know how long he had been running for, all he knew was that he didn't want to stop. Bradford thought he had run a mile or two. In reality it was only a block, but it was the most that Bradford had ever run because on Fridays when they ran the mile first thing in the morning, he made sure to be tardy. Of course, that meant his P.E. grade was a fail, but at least his other grades were all A++. He saw a deserted alleyway and hopped in a nearby trashcan.

He felt sticky and noticed his pajama top was soaked with yellow paint. He also felt as if he was missing something, but what could it be? Before he could think about what was missing, he heard a croaky laugh and hopped out of his shoes.

*Was it the demon teachers?* So many thoughts raced through his head, will he die? He hadn't even asked Miranda on a date yet.

But before he could think of any other negative thoughts, he heard the school principal, Mr. Gramber.

"It's breakfast time," he snarled.

*Great now even the principal is a demon, and I'm*

*about to die.*

Bradford leaped out of the trashcan, slipped on a pomegranate peel, and continued to slide right through Mr. Gramber's legs. Instead of a catchy escape like in the movies, Bradford just laid there and realized that not all stunts in movies can be replicated in real life. He asserted a few choice words in his mind, accompanied by a long noisy groan, and he knew he was done for.

He attempted to get up on his feet but fell again. As he opened his eyes, he expected to see Mr. Gramber's short, hunchback, meager body hovering over him, laughing and sharpening his nails.

Bradford's expectation was correct as he heard Mr. Gramber's croaky laugh.

"Well, look who we have here. Jimmy, I always knew you were a troublemaker. Luckily for you, you will never fail a test again or ever attempt to pass one, but who are we kidding? That's an impossible feat for you."

*Jimmy? Who was Jimmy?* Bradford thought.

Then Bradford realized what he was missing. It was his glasses. He only needed them for reading and seeing far distances. Fortunately, he could see objects right in front of him. As Bradford stared at Mr. Gramber's glistening nails, he saw his own reflection. Without glasses, Bradford looked unrecognizable. It was also fortunate that Bradford was not wearing his pinstriped suit, which would be a dead giveaway. That was why Mr. Gramber thought he was a boy named Jimmy. Not wearing his glasses or pinstriped suit helped hide Bradford's identity from the villainous school principal.

"And we educators will eat like royalty today with your help, of course, Jimmy," Mr. Gramber blabbered on, but that wasn't what Bradford was focused on. He was plotting a plan that could potentially save his life.

Bradford was sort of mischievous in elementary school, which is ironic seeing what a goody two shoes he was now.

Whenever Bradford was in trouble in elementary school, he would yell, "Look behind you. It's your mom!" When the kids would stop in their tracks and look over their shoulder, Bradford would snicker and scatter away. This seemed to be the best course of action to escape, considering he always had a shrimpy stature.

Bradford had a flashback and laughed beneath his breath. He felt a childish mischievous sensation and didn't feel like the 14-year-old junior in high school who was studying for the SATs and AP tests every second of the day. Rather, he felt like a second grader with no worries in life except to enjoy his years of freedom and childhood. And he also felt the gratifying sensation of laughing non-stop. In other words, Bradford felt like a second grader and was about to act like one.

There is a time and place for everything. There are times when you shouldn't do something, and there are times when you should do something. For example, if you're accepted into your dream college, you shouldn't enroll in a community college, and you should accept enrollment into your dream college as it may be a once in a lifetime opportunity. Another example is you shouldn't slap your younger brother in front of your parents as you will get into trouble, but you should kick him under the table so you will get away with it. However, no, please don't do that. One last example is you shouldn't go into your teachers' conference room and start dancing on the table or else they may do a duet with you and not in a pleasant way, and you should move to Afghanistan if your teachers and school principal are evil demons trying to devour you alive. In Bradford's case, you shouldn't act like a second grader in a life or death situation because second graders are immature and usually don't make sound decisions, and you should make a mature and calculated move.

Bradford stared Mr. Gramber in the eyes, pointed behind him, and blurted out "Oh, look, it's your mom!"

Mr. Gramber looked behind him, and Bradford bolted. He couldn't believe a second-grade mentality can outwit a demon principal. While running toward the streets, Bradford could have sworn he saw the outline of a car—after all, he didn't have his glasses—and went straight toward the object, hollering to stop and let him in. The car came to a screeching halt. Bradford noticed the front passenger window was open. It was his only chance, so he jumped and dove in. Before his legs were inside the car, he felt the sudden jerk of the car lunging forward. Bradford managed to curl into a ball and secure his legs inside the car, and as he looked to see who his savior was, he was surprised to see Maverick at the wheel, driving full speed.

His friends hadn't abandoned him! He looked back and saw Andy and Miranda smiling at him while Spike glared at him as if he was mad that Bradford was safe and wished he had died.

Bradford was bombarded with questions and sighs of relief from everyone except Spike. They were all very curious about what happened to him, and Bradford didn't spare any details. He explained everything, starting with Mr. Abram knowing his identity, how he hid under a floorboard, oddly located in the bushes, while the teachers argued how they could order squirrels as an early morning snack and finally how Mr. Gramber thought he was Jimmy.

After Bradford explained everything to his friends, Maverick stated, "Well, if Mr. Gramber thought you were Jimmy, then I guess we'd better get you new glasses and a pinstripe suit. Otherwise, we don't know what may happen to you if you're mistaken for another kid because soon enough Mr. Gramber will figure out you're not Jimmy and hunt you down."

"We'd better get to it because school is starting in exactly one hour and forty-eight minutes," Andy said, and they headed off into the distance.

I wish I could say they drove to the airport

and moved to Afghanistan, and hung out with snow leopards and Asiatic black bears, but not all stories end with happy endings, and not all stories end up in Afghanistan.

"Where will we find glasses and a pinstriped suit?" questioned Miranda.

"We'll figure that out later," responded Maverick.

"When is later?" Miranda sighed as she shook her head.

She looked so beautiful that Bradford started staring and drooling simultaneously. Yes, it was a weird sight to see, a boy smelling like trash and looking like he was hit with the world's largest paintball who only cared about one thing and that was staring at this one girl.

"Bradford, where can we go to get you new clothes and glasses?" Miranda inquired.

*Snap out of it!* he told himself. Instead of saying, "Let's swing by my house," Bradford responded by saying, "We can go to the mall that never closes. I should be able to purchase glasses and clothes there." He tried to sound as cool as he could even though he looked like a ginormous golden grape and smelled like spoiled onions.

"The twenty-four-hour mall it is!" Maverick shouted.

But let me tell you, they wouldn't sound this excited for long.

# CHAPTER 4: SQUIRRELS! SQUIRRELS! OH, YEAH, AND SQUIRRELS!

T he drive to the mall was uneventful. There were no hardships or earthquakes swallowing them up from beneath the ground. They arrived at the mall that never closes, but no one was there. There were no employees or customers, but the store doors were wide open.

"This is very odd," Maverick announced suspiciously.

Then lightning struck. BANG! Bradford was spooked, but he told himself, *It's just lightning.* He shrugged it off and kept on truckin' as if nothing had ever happened. He then realized everything was dead silent. He looked behind him in the hopes of spotting his friends, but they had disappeared into thin air yet again. However, he was not alone. Right in front of him, he saw something, which would scar him for life. He saw… the squirrels.

"What is this? The three musketeers plus a spare?" Bradford mumbled. Then all the lights went out, and Bradford bellowed, "Where are my friends? Maverick? Miranda? Andy?"

Notice how he excluded Spike as he did not consider him a friend.

"Oh, your friends are irrelevant," a high-pitched voice said, snickering.

"Who are you?" Bradford shouted into the darkness.

"Oh, you know." Announced another high-pitched voice, giggling.

"Show yourself. I'm not afraid to hurt you, you, whoever you are!" Bradford stated.

"We're right here!" Screamed four little voices.

"Where?" Bradford questioned.

"Literally right below you." One of the voices sighed.

"What?" Bradford asked.

"Why does this always happen to us? Whenever we try to sound evil, everyone is like 'Where are you?' Squirrels from Morocco, who traveled here by donkey, on a pirate ship, are very scary okay!"

As the lights turned back on, Bradford realized the squirrels were the ones talking.

"Oh, yeah, sure, very very scary," Bradford sarcastically answered. "Now that we got that over with, can you tell me where my friends are?"

he asked without questioning how these squirrels could speak.

The squirrels erupted in what was supposed to be an evil laughter, but it really sounded like a dying frog in the middle of labor, who had just inhaled helium with pepper spray in its eyes. And yes, I've encountered one before. I wouldn't categorize it as a pleasant sight.

"You can have your friends back on one condition. You will give us what we want," one of the squirrels announced.

"What condition?" Bradford curiously asked.

"We want the power inside of you. Why else would those teachers want to hunt you down? Besides, if you don't give us your power, the teachers will take it themselves in the most horrific manner," one of the squirrels stated as if possessed.

"What are you talking about? I have no power. I'm just tremendously smart. There are nerds everywhere, so why pick on me?" Bradford asked.

"Because you're the smartest person ever to live. All of the IQ tests assess your IQ score at a whopping 468. That's 205 IQ points higher than Ainan Celeste Cawley, who was in first place until you surpassed his score by almost two times."

At that moment, Bradford's jaw dropped. 468? That was impossible and crazy in every way imaginable. Bradford knew he was smart but not that smart.

Then the squirrels, as if they were possessed,

started to perform a ritual. Their eyes fell out of their sockets, and they started jumping around in a tribal circle. As lightning struck, they started chanting...

*Mother Nature, you're so wise. Mother Nature, we're in awe. Mother Nature, you bond us all. Mother Nature, until the end of time. Mother Nature, you're so strong. Mother Nature, you can conquer all."*

At that moment, Bradford dashed off. He didn't want to be near these crazed entranced squirrels, and he hoped that the teachers would get hungry and hunt the squirrels down. Bradford didn't know which way to run. All he wanted to do was escape. He had forgotten why he came to the mall in the first place, and he just wanted to find his friends and get the hell out of there. As he ran forward to what seemed to be more mall space, he hit his head on a sign that appeared out of nowhere, causing him to fall onto the ground and injure his left hand. His hand was throbbing at full tilt from the fall and he prayed it wasn't broken.

He was starting to panic, but he told himself, *Stay strong. It's just a game. These crazy teachers are playing mind tricks.*

He then yelled, "Show yourself, teachers, or whoever you are. If you think you are smart enough to outwit me, you are dead wrong."

Bradford had no idea what he was saying. He was trying to intimidate the teachers, telling them that he knows this is their evil plot to scare him and that he's not rattled by them. Deep down, to the contrary, Bradford's real state of mind was sheer panic. In his mind, he was thinking, *What is happening? I need my mom. I think I may have soiled my pants.*

Then he heard some chattering, like a high-pitched laugh with a squeal.

He murmured to himself, "Alvin and the Chipmunks, is that you?"

And then Bradford collapsed. His hand and head stopped throbbing as he smashed into the concrete floor below him. His whole body went numb, like a power off button on your phone.

When he opened his eyes, everything was a blinding white. Bradford saw his father, who had died a couple of months ago. Bradford extended his arm out for him, but he couldn't reach him. All he saw was his father's loving smile, the smile that was engraved in his memory. As he was about to yell for his dad, a black abyss sucked his dad away.

A hissing laughter exclaimed, "You can only get your father back under one condition."

Then Bradford yelled, "What condition? I'll do anything! I promise. Just tell me!"

When Bradford came to, he saw sixty eyes focused on him, but they weren't squirrels. They were his classmates, and he was somehow back in his AP Calculus class. Then his eyes shifted to Mr. Abram whose fists were clenched, nose was flared out, and cheeks were flushed.

"What do you think you're doing, mister?" Mr. Abram questioned.

Was this all a dream? Could it be that Bradford had dozed off in sixth period, and the past twenty-four hours never happened? After all, his hand and head no longer ached, and he was wearing his pin-stripe suit and glasses. The next five minutes of class felt like an eternity, Bradford couldn't wait to bolt out of class, dash home, and put this whole bazaar dream behind him, but Bradford would not be that lucky.

"Bradford stay after class. We have to have a brief chat," Mr. Abram stated with a sly grin on his face.

Usually staying after class is for something beneficial. If your grade is suffering and you need some extra tutoring, then you may stay after class to learn more about the subject and improve your grade, or if a raw fish is stuck in your shoe, maybe your teacher will make you stay after class to teach you something really boring to make the fish jump out of your shoe and leap out the boring classroom window. In Bradford's case, staying afterschool was a complete nightmare!

"Bradford, please close the door," Mr. Abram ordered.

"Uh-huh, no problemo," Bradford replied as he shut the door.

"So, Bradford, why were you yelling in class?" Mr. Abram questioned.

"I was only daydreaming. Nothing much. It won't happen again," Bradford said.

Mr. Abram started pacing the room, inspecting Bradford as if he was an important piece of clue in solving a murder mystery plot.

"Just daydreaming?" Mr. Abram questioned with a smirk plastered on his face. "You know, I lost my father at a young age, too. It was devastating. I couldn't connect with my mom, so I disposed of her. She was irrelevant."

"How did you know about my dream?" Bradford asked while backing up.

"Oh, I know everything Bradford," Mr. Abram replied as a hysterical smile spread across his face.

Bradford didn't think this was funny, so he galloped towards the door. The doorknob wouldn't budge. While in the haste of trying to unlock the door, Bradford felt a searing pain course through his left hand again, and he knew this was no nightmare. He let out a startled yelp as Mr. Abram approached him slowly but surely. Bradford was struck with panic, and he was scared to death. I mean, he wasn't sure. Maybe death was approaching as Mr. Abram's steps got closer and closer. He didn't know what to do. He then stared at the second story window. He took a deep breath and mustered up all his courage, and he bolted straight towards the open window and jumped through it. Bradford did not expect to experience what happened next. As he was plummeting to his death, he felt a blanket of warm fur soften his blow. Then he looked down and saw that it was the squirrels. Those crazy creatures saved his life!

"Oh, Bradford, those one-off nightmares in

your head will go away one day. Soon your entire life will be one giant nightmare!" Mr. Abram shouted to Bradford.

Bradford was stunned. His brain couldn't process everything that was happening. Where were his friends? How did he get from the mall to math class? How did he acquire the new glasses and pinstriped suit? What did Mr. Abram mean by 'one giant nightmare'? Did he just bust through a second story window like a cool action superhero? Lastly, did he just face death only to be saved by squirrels? As he got his bearings, Bradford realized lying on a sea of squirrels was uncomfortable, so he rolled off his furry security blank.

Bradford was about to run back home, but Mr. Abram's voice stopped him in his tracks.

"Oh, Bradford, it's pathetic that you, a classified genius, can't figure out what's happening. Oh, but don't worry your little heart out, you will figure it out soon, very very very soon."

Bradford was curious, so he circled back around and hopped in a nearby dumpster. Although this wasn't one of the smartest moments in Bradford's lifetime, it was for sure one of the most courageous moments. Sadly, most courageous people die.

"Bradford, you think home is safe. Well, not anymore. You will have some visitors waiting for you," a voice murmured above him.

Did Bradford hear that correct? What did the voice mean when he murmured his home isn't safe? Were the teachers going to kill him in his own home? Bradford just sat in the grimy, stench-filled dumpster, all alone with no one to hug him or console him. He continued sitting in the smelly germ-infested dumpster, wishing he were dumb. He would have never wished that before, but now he was being hunted by demon teachers because he was too smart and he had nowhere to run to, even his home wasn't safe. Bradford wished he could be anywhere else and doing anything else other than live this nightmare.

"I guess it can't get much worse," Bradford mumbled to himself.

Little did Bradford know; it would get much worse.

# CHAPTER 5: I MAKE FRIENDS WITH A SQUIRREL

Bradford sat in the dumpster for hours and hours. It was now close to midnight since it was pitch black outside. Bradford could hear the growling of his stomach as he hadn't eaten anything for over a day. He finally started to doze off until he felt something grazing his right shoulder. He looked up quickly.

"Oh, hi, squirrel," Bradford grumbled and started to close his eyes again. "Wait! Why are you here?"

"I wanted to wish you goodnight," the squirrel said with a smile.

"You're not my mom. Go away!" Bradford snapped and shoved the squirrel away.

Bradford was sad because this squirrel was so much like a parent, the soft smile on his face, him saying goodnight and making sure he was safe.

The squirrel nodded his head and scurried away with his head hanging low. Every step the squirrel took made Bradford's eyes tear up. He felt the one thing that cared for him now was escaping his grasp. He couldn't let this opportunity pass him by.

Bradford had made many mistakes in his life, and he didn't want this to be one of his highlights. He glanced back at the squirrel and bellowed, "Hey! Come back!"

The squirrel turned his head in Bradford's direction and stopped in his tracks, not moving a muscle. The squirrel looked straight into Bradford's eyes as if he was inspecting every aspect of Bradford's being.

"Sorry for the misunderstanding a minute ago. I'm just overwhelmed that you care about me. I'm very sorry, and I hope you will accept my apology," Bradford said.

"It's fine," the squirrel responded with a shrug. "I know how tough your situation is, and I wanted to help you. Maybe we can be like Batman and Robin. We can stop the evil force of Malinfesa!" the squirrel announced with a triumphant look on his face.

"Malinfesa? What does that even mean? That sounds like a biology or chemistry term or possibly an Egyptian mythology phrase," Bradford said.

"You don't know?" the squirrel stated, genuinely confused.

"I have no idea what Malinfesa means," Bradford replied to the squirrel.

The squirrel let out a long groan. "You've totally ruined the heroic moment. We were supposed to burst out of this dumpster and save your friends."

"My friends? Where are they? I need to know!" Bradford leaned in towards the squirrel.

"I will tell you, but you're smart enough to know that the teachers aren't stupid. They will be expecting you. Now sit!" the squirrel ordered with such confidence that Bradford felt he had to oblige.

"Okay, what's your name? I need to know what to call you," Bradford said.

"Call me A.K. Squirrels don't have names. We only have initials," A.K. responded.

"Alright, A.K., tell me more about the curse of Malinfesa," Bradford exclaimed.

"If you insist. The curse of Malinfesa is a curse which chases and captures the smartest people around the world. The curse has been around since the beginning of time. Every century, the curse surfaces and finds its newest victim, and now, you are number one on the list."

"If the curse is after me, why were so many kids captured before me?" questioned Bradford.

"After being dormant for 100 years, when the curse resurfaces, it needs to capture and kill hosts to build its strength and become powerful. The curse can also possess people close to you, who can earn your trust and capture you. In short, the curse doesn't just affect you, but all parties involved. The curse has taken over your teachers' souls and has turned them into evil cannibalistic demons. We squirrels have been working tirelessly against this curse since the beginning of time. This is why squirrels were created. The curse is after you because you are the smartest person ever to live, and if Malinfesa possesses your intellect, doomsday will come."

Bradford asked, "How do we stop this curse?"

"No one knows for sure. It's never been done before, and I must warn you. This feat is nearly impossible to accomplish. We have seen the best of the best defeated and destroyed by Malinfesa, but you Bradford, you are special. You have the eternal force to stop the curse of Malinfesa once and for all!" A.K. stated. "But fail and the world will end as we know it."

"Okay, this is like a tragic movie. Generation after generation are failing to defeat the curse, and then you're told you have the eternal force. Now go and complete the impossible task at hand or else the world will self-destruct," Bradford said with no enthusiasm whatsoever.

"That's basically it," A.K. confirmed.

"Did I ever sign a contract for this? No. So, can't I just walk away and when the curse comes after me, lawyer up?" Bradford questioned.

"They said you were smart. The curse doesn't care about contracts or lawyers. It takes you either way unless you can stop it," A.K. announced.

"Fine, let's go save my friends wherever they are," Bradford replied. He was still disgruntled about the fact that there was no contract for this deadly mission.

"So, your friends are somewhere on the right side of the school," A.K. said.

"AAAAAAAAAAAAH!" A girl's scream was heard from the left side of the school.

"Correction, they are on the left side of the school," A.K. responded.

"What are we waiting for? Let's go save my friends!" Bradford hurried in the direction of the scream. "Are you coming?" Bradford looked back at A.K.

"Does Batman go anywhere without Robin?" A.K. replied with a grin from ear to ear.

"Yeah, they probably don't go to the restroom together, but that's beside the point. Hurry up. We've got to go!" Bradford replied.

A.K. let out a chuckle and followed Bradford to the door. That short moment of enjoyment was ruined when they heard that terrible scream again. Bradford realized it was Miranda screaming.

"A.K., hop on my shoulder. It's war time now!" Bradford stated, anger boiling inside him, which he wanted to unleash badly.

"Whatever you say boss," A.K. replied.

A.K. hopped on Bradford's shoulders, and they sprinted towards the terrifying scream.

Usually, when you learn your teachers are demons, which we can all obviously relate to, at some point in our lives, and hear terrifying screams, you probably should run away, not run towards the commotion. Of course, Miranda was Bradford's friend, and he had a crush on her, but still it was a terrible decision. It's as dumb of a decision as letting your dog, who you were about to drive to the vet, take control of the wheel. It doesn't turn out well. Actually, it leads to eternal darkness—a.k.a. death.

Bradford sprinted through the dark halls. They went on forever, longer than usual. How did he get from class to class with these never-ending halls? The darkness seemed to be consuming him alive and whole. He was starting to think he should turn back, but he was determined. He was as determined as a toddler who just wanted the cookie from the cookie jar that he could barely reach. Then Bradford heard the screams again. It was non-stop screaming, but now it sounded more like a hysterical laughter, an evil type of laughter, a laugh that makes your skin crawl and a laugh that's basically announcing you are stuck in my trap and you will never escape. The hallway never ended, but Bradford kept running and running with A.K. planted firmly on his shoulder while getting absolutely nowhere. However, the noises kept getting louder and louder as if they were getting closer. The farther he ran, the dimmer the lights became. Every door was closed shut. While looking for somewhere to go, Bradford saw a peculiar door. This door was different from the rest. It had an illuminating purple glow outlining it and a sign with carved letters.

"A.K., look at this door. Do you see the purple glow and the carvings?" Bradford asked in a hushed tone.

"I don't see anything. Why?" A.K. replied, whispering.

"The door says something on it," Bradford replied.

"I don't know if you have super vision power, but I don't see anything. That door is the same as any other door," A.K. replied, confused.

"It reads, 'Detention'. Wait, what happened? The screaming stopped," Bradford whispered.

"There is only one thing to do, and that is to barge in," A.K. replied.

Bradford hesitated. This was probably one of the dumbest decisions in his lifetime. When you are being chased by a curse, which is trying to steal your soul and bring the world to an end and has recruited your teachers to act as demons, you probably shouldn't go into a room with illuminating lights and a sign that reads, 'Detention'. After all, detention is where you are punished for your actions. Although Bradford did nothing wrong, he was facing the consequences of what detention would be but a few trillion times worse. Bradford was about to say, "We should get out of here," when he heard a creaking noise of a chair. It had to be Andy! Bradford and Andy had made a secret code, consisting of squeaking noises. Bradford put his index finger on his lips, signing to be quiet, as A.K. leapt off his shoulder.

Bradford heard a creak noise, which was code for the letter "C". After that, he heard a stomp noise, which signaled the letter "O". He then heard the noise of a shoe tapping, which meant the letter "M". Lastly, he heard a "keeeeer" noise signaling an "E". "COME." Bradford then heard the muffled scream of

Andy. He figured this meant "Come help".

Bradford turned to A.K. and nodded, which signaled they were going in.

If you think this scene ends in cupcakes and rainbows, then you probably think Bradford busted the door open and heroically saved his friends with ease.

Sadly, life is not that simple. Going back to Agnies Academy, Bradford's high school, to trace his footsteps, I can only speak the truth. If you don't want the truth, then I advise you to close this book right now. If you want to imagine Bradford saving his friends with ease, you're better off reading a Disney book.

If you're still here reading more about Bradford's depressing reality, I will now tell you what really happened. Bradford opened the door slowly and cowardly. After all, not all geniuses are courageous. The door let out a long creak, and Bradford saw an image of three people in chairs. All three of them had gags in their mouths, and each one was tied to a chair. Bradford felt a sharp pain through his entire body, and everything went black.

# CHAPTER 6: WHAT DID I JUST WITNESS?

**W**hen Bradford came to, he was tied up, and A.K. was nowhere in sight. A voice zinged in his ear, "Well, well, well, look what the cat drug in. How exciting is this?" Mr. Abram laughed, like a pack of hyenas.

"Muy emocionada!" Mrs. Ramirez responded with a mile to mile grin across her face.

"What's going on?" Bradford asked with a puzzled look on his face.

"Brrrrrr!" a muffled voice echoed.

Bradford rotated his head clockwise and saw it was Miranda.

*Oh, you're trying to say some demonic teachers kidnapped us and are watching us suffer for their own sick pleasure. That explains a lot. I now see why kids think teachers are evil. The pieces fit perfectly together,* Bradford thought.

He then reminded himself, *Wait, it's not the teachers' fault. They're under the curse of Malinfesa.*

"Smarty pants say adios. This may be your final moments," Mrs. Ramirez said, snickering as she addressed Bradford with an evil tint in her eyes.

Realizing he was about to die, Bradford's adrenaline shot right through the roof as he felt a weird sensation thrust up his spine and give his brain a new jolt of energy. He felt like an abandoned robot who was inactive for decades and then replenished with a top of the line battery pack with a 102 percent charging capacity. His eyes started bulging as if they were about to burst out of their sockets. *Is this a supernatural power, like the one the Incredible Hulk possesses?* Bradford questioned. From all the books he had read, in do or die situations, the protagonist always survives. Then he heard a faint voice in his head, one which was speaking in a whisper.

*Bradford, listen up. Otherwise, you're going to be barbequed alive, which probably won't be the most pleasant sensation to encounter,"* the voice whispered as if he talked any louder, all his friends would die.

Bradford scanned the room with his eyes for any clues as to where the voice may be originating from. He first inspected Miranda, went past Maverick, Andy, Mrs. Ramirez, and the other teachers, and saw no clues that would indicate the voice was coming from one of them. In the darkness behind Mr. Abram, he noticed was a boy who was hunched over, looking at the ground and filled with extreme guilt.

*Wait, it's Spike, that little rascal. He's been conspiring with the teachers all along!* Bradford thought.

Spike avoided eye contact as he was getting the look of death from all his friends.

"Spike, don't hide, you snake!" Bradford shouted, trying to sound confident.

"Does it matter what he is? I'm pretty sure I know what he is and that he is not dead. You four, however, will be dead in a matter of a couple of minutes. We plan to barbecue you during our teacher bonding time!" Mr. Abram retorted with excitement in his voice.

"Oh, don't get ahead of yourself!" a voice shouted from behind the door.

Bradford recognized the voice! He just couldn't put his finger on it, but he figured it out in about 1.79 seconds as 400 squirrels busted their way through the door, yelling, with A.K. in the lead. Bradford was so relieved that A.K. didn't bail out of fear, but rather he bailed out of necessity to bring reinforcement.

"Charge, brothers! Cut their ropes!" A.K. yelled, a glimmer of light streaking across his eyes as if his eyes were shooting stars.

If shooting stars were darting out of A.K.'s eyes, Bradford's wish came true, being saved right in the nick of time.

The best part about the ambush was that it wasn't an attack. Out of pure fright, the teachers retreated, leaped up into the air, and plastered themselves against the ceiling. I guess they hadn't had their rabies shot. On the other hand, Spike was stranded on the ground, feverishly backing up into a corner and screaming for his mommy. Bradford couldn't hold a small chuckle from escaping his mouth. Bradford looked at A.K., and he gave him a small wink and a slight grin.

"Get to untying the children!" A.K. yelled at the other squirrels as if he was the only male lion in the pack or as if he was an eagle in a flock of pigeons.

The squirrels swarmed around the room like a school of magnificent brown fish, weaving through human legs and each other. They were so in sync that it seemed as if they had been practicing for this moment for the past century. They jumped over and slid under each other like they were in a military training course and were ultra-determined to complete their mission or as if they were in the Olympics, sprinting for the gold medal. With his inquisitive mind, Bradford noticed all these inferences in a matter of two seconds.

He also noticed Mr. Abram gazing at A.K. with murder in his eyes as if A.K. had slaughtered his loved ones and made him watch. Mr. Abram started to flap his arms like they were wings and swooped down on his prey. Bradford felt an unknown strength surge through his body and in and out of his bones. He somehow managed to rip his constraints off and dove towards Mr. Abram, who was inching closer and closer towards A.K. Everything seemed to move in slow motion. A.K. watched in terror as Mr. Abram opened his mouth and brought his sharp fangs closer and closer towards him. Bradford, still midair, reached out and grabbed his furry friend to safety just in the nick of time. Mr. Abram was so close to devouring A.K. as if he was the turkey at Thanksgiving dinner. Mr. Abram missed A.K. but instead managed to puncture a hole in Bradford's shoe, causing him to lose his balance.

As Bradford felt the pavement beneath him, he was engulfed with a jolt of pain that bolted through his body, and he screamed bloody murder. The pain overtook Bradford's body, and his arms rotated like helicopter propellers, slashing Mr. Abram all over his body and causing him to fly airborne. Once he regained control of his arms, Bradford scanned the room to see where Mr. Abram landed. He finally located his math teacher sprawled on the floor and knocked out cold. His long vampire fangs sprung out from his mouth and slid across the room. In desperation, Bradford crawled over to Mr. Abram to check for a pulse. Thankfully, he was still alive.

Bradford then felt nothing. Where had Mr. Abram gone? He couldn't have just vanished. Bradford then spotted a hole in the ground, an inch to his left. Mr. Abram must have fell through it. This stupid curse was causing so many problems for Bradford, and now it was killing people. Bradford desperately looked down the hole. At first, he only saw darkness and nothing else. This couldn't be. Where was Mr. Abram? Then he spotted him about thirty feet below, dangling by a thread from a piece of wood. Bradford saw his eyes flutter open in confusion, looking around in fear. Mr. Abram looked like a baby bird surrounded by a pack of wolves.

"Mr. Abram, we'll save you. Hang in there!"

Bradford said.

"Why? He's trying to kill us!" an angry voice behind him demanded.

Bradford whipped around to see Andy, Maverick, and Miranda next to him. They were so relieved to be free from their gags and constraints but still shaken up and startled from almost being killed.

"Are you going to answer us?" Miranda snapped.

"It's just not right to let him die." Bradford answered.

"He doesn't deserve our mercy!" Maverick stated.

"It's not his fault! A curse called Malinfesa has taken over him, causing him to be an evil demon. If you don't want to help, then leave!" Bradford yelled at Maverick.

"Fine, dude. We'll help but only because we owe it to you for saving our lives." Maverick answered.

"Mr. Abram, can you fly?" Bradford asked.

"Bradford, that is nonsense. You're the smartest person in the world. You know I can't fly. My expertise is calculus," Mr. Abram responded.

"But? He's now normal again. The spell has been broken," Bradford said, relieved.

He then noticed a purple figure zoom out from Mr. Abram's mouth and through the window towards the sky.

"What was that? And better yet why am I dangling by a thread off this piece of wood and about to fall to my death. Wait… AAAAAAH, SOME-ONE HELP ME!" Mr. Abram screeched.

"Oh, Bradford, don't worry. The curse just left his soul. You still have us to deal with. It will be so exciting!" Coach Rogers said.

"HELP ME!" Mr. Abram yelled, sounding like a toddler who had just gotten her bright pink balloon and favorite princess doll stuck in a tree.

Again, I advise you to close this book right now. In doing so, you may think Bradford easily destroyed the curse, saving everyone, including Mr. Abram, who was holding on to life by a thread, both literally and metaphorically. If you are still reading, then you may witness catastrophe firsthand. Sounds fun, right?

As Bradford was reaching his hand down into complete darkness, he heard a cracking noise and then a human scream. This was a scream of none other than his teacher, Mr. Abram. Bradford watched as he saw his math teacher plummet towards a dark, scary, dismal, and dreary abyss. His voice slowly faded away until there was utter silence. Bradford felt a pat on his back. It was A.K. He was like a father figure to Bradford, and he was always there when he needed him most.

"It's too late now. I'm sorry, Bradford," A.K. announced in a defeated tone.

Bradford grimaced knowing the sad truth that it was too late to save Mr. Abram. After hearing creaking floorboards, Barford realized that except for A.K., all the squirrels had disappeared. Their reinforcements had abandoned them. As he turned around, Mrs. Ramirez, no longer plastered to the ceiling, was hovering behind him.

"Hola, amiga!" Mrs. Ramirez shouted in glee, as she extended her arm to push Miranda into eternal darkness.

Bradford's adrenaline kicked into overdrive as he felt the same surge of energy he had felt earlier when he was tied up and had to save A.K. He leapt toward Mrs. Ramirez to prevent her from killing Miranda. He zoned in on Mrs. Ramirez and scanned her from head to toe. He studied her entire body in a matter of seconds, finding her vulnerable body parts. Her legs were the most vulnerable from many years of walking in the school halls and getting accidently kicked or tripped by objects laying on the floor. Bradford grabbed a hold of her left thigh and while in the air, kicked her right leg from underneath her. Mrs. Ramirez fell onto her back and knocked Miranda to safety, barely missed falling in the bottomless pit herself.

Knowing the other teachers would pursue them, Bradford firmly commanded his friends to clear out and led by running through the detention room door he had originally entered before this entire fiasco began. Although it was exhilarating running for his life, it was not the triumph he yearned for, but he had an inclination, a.k.a. gut feeling, that victory would prevail in the end.

"Bradford, come back! You don't want to ruin your perfect attendance record. Your grades will drop like the jocks, and it would be a shame for you not to be valedictorian next year," Mrs. Bloomer shouted after him.

Bradford started to turn around, but Andy stopped him in his tracks.

"Keep your eyes on the ultimate prize, which is escaping these cannibalistic teachers. Otherwise, we are all going to die. I know it hurts you, Bradford, but this is what is the best for all of us. If you want to live to see yourself attending Harvard, this is the only way," Andy said.

"You're right," Bradford replied. "Thank you for knocking some sense into me."

"Anytime, I know you would do the same for me," Andy stated. "Let's focus on what's important. You don't want your fate to be like Mr. Abram's." Bradford nodded and kept running.

# CHAPTER 7: HEALTH OFFICE? MORE LIKE DEATH OFFICE

Thump. Thump. Thump.

"Where are we?" Bradford questioned.

There were no more doors, just hallway walls, there was nothing but walls.

"Wait up, guys. Stop running. Let's find out where we are," Maverick said.

"There is no telling where we are now," Miranda responded in a lost voice.

"We can still slow down, catch our breath, and try to find where we are," Maverick said.

"Good idea. Let's just walk the rest of the way. Your feet are much bigger than mine," A.K. said.

"Wait, what's that?" Bradford questioned.

"I'm never getting a break." A.K. sighed.

"Do you not see that door?" Bradford asked, pointing towards the door right next to them.

"What door? Bradford, you need to take a break. You're probably hallucinating. You just need to take a break," Miranda stated.

"No, I'm going through the door. I don't know about you guys," Bradford said.

Prior to entering, Bradford noticed a plaque above the door. He wiped off the dirt and grime with his forearm and made out the words, "Health Office".

"Oh, no," Bradford murmured.

"What is it?" Maverick asked.

"We need to enter. It could give us answers," Bradford replied. And without waiting for his friends to respond, he barged through the door.

Upon entering the Health Office, unaccompanied by his friends, Bradford was met by an astonishing figure with a translucent physique of a middle-aged man, lounging in a chair; surrounded by frozen children as if they were dead. WAIT, they were dead! Chills rushed down Bradford's spine. He had the urge to run back out the door, but he had a feeling, a feeling of unfinished business.

*Unfinished business is probably discarding my remains after I'm murdered,* Bradford thought.

"Well, well, look who finally decided to grace us with his presence. Bradford, I have been expecting you. Come, come, come." the man addressed Bradford with his dilated eyes and semitransparent mangled body, radiating a glowing green tint.

"And no, you can't leave until you answer my riddles. If you answer all of the riddles correctly, you will hear your prophecy and can leave," the man said, scowling as if he knew he was about to add another body to his morbid collection.

"How did you read my mind about wanting to leave?" Bradford questioned.

"I know many things about you, child. You seem dissatisfied as if you are a stray soul wandering around the Fields of Punishments in the Underworld, terrified, hungry, and desperate for freedom, love, and redemption. But you will have to solve the riddles in exchange for your freedom. If you fail, you will pay with your life," the figure informed Bradford nonchalantly with a villainous grin taped across his distorted face.

"What if—" Bradford started to ask.

"No, you have to answer the three riddles," the voice interjected.

Bradford's heart was beating louder than a pack of fanatic fans watching the NBA finals as their underdog team scored a buzzer beater for the win. Although his heart was beating exponentially louder than the fans of the winning team, he felt the feeling of defeat and frustration for the losing team at the same time. What did he do to get himself into this predicament? He had never wanted to be a part of this. Why did he have to be so smart?

He goggled at the bodies sprawled on the floor. He realized the odd and bothersome noises, which resembled faint cries followed by gritty laughter that he initially heard before barging into the bathroom where he had first met Miranda, were coming from here. They were the cries of kids dying and this man's demented laughter.

He saw his classmates. Some of the other

smartest kids in the school. There was Derrick from his calculus class, Dorothy from his AP physics class, and so many other decaying and decayed bodies. Some of their flesh were decomposing while others were bare-bones, probably students from centuries ago. Agnies Academy was very old, but Bradford never expected it to be this ancient. He could not believe his eyes and could have sworn his heart jumped out of his throat.

"Don't croak on me now, Bradford. The time will come soon enough, but meanwhile, let's have some fun!" the man said.

"Dorothy and Derrick were both at school yesterday. Their bodies couldn't have possibly decayed so rapidly within less than two days," Bradford muttered, confused.

"Those are just clones. We have to replenish part of the school population. Otherwise, how do you think we'll keep it on the down low? If we killed every student in the school and announced they must have vanished into thin air, this school would be overrun and destroyed in 2.2 seconds by those low-down homicidal mothers. After all, they're the fiercest creatures of all times. Trust me, I speak from experience. Anyway, that's beside the point. Let's not get sidetracked. It's trivia time. And your host is...yours truly, the iniquitous, a.k.a. evil son of Malinfesa. The price if you get any of these three riddles wrong is...DEATH! On the other hand, if you get them all right, you get to escape with your life in your hands and a prophecy that may defeat my dear symbolic mother, Malinfesa, who has granted me immortality so long as no one solves my riddles. Now, can I get a round of applause? No? That's fine. Suit yourself. Anyway, Bradford, are you ready? Good, because ready or not, here we go!" the curse's symbolic son said as if he was Steve Harvey, announcing a new episode of *Family Feud*.

"Ask away," Bradford replied, trying to sound confident even though he was scared to the bones. "By the way, what is your name?"

"Mallard," the voice responded, confused by Bradford's question and enthusiasm. "Anyways, first question, If you have me, you want to share me. If you share me, you haven't got me. What am I?"

"If you have me, you want to share me," Bradford mumbled under his breath.

*What could it be? Bradford thought. It could be your abilities or talents, but it could also be a secret. The rest states, 'If you share me, you haven't gotten me'. If you share your talents, you don't lose it, but you lose a secret when you share it because it isn't a secret anymore!*

"A secret!" Bradford announced.

"Final answer?" Mallard smiled as if he had just added another corpse to his collection.

Bradford studied Mallard's facial expression. His eyeballs seemed to be a bit enlarged as if he was awestruck. Bradford discerned, a.k.a. perceived, that Mallard's smile was a bluff to throw Bradford off guard.

"Yes, a secret is my final answer," Bradford intrepidly, in other words, bravely, answered.

"Sadly, Bradford, you are correct." Mallard sighed, a deep frown indented on his forehead, which slowly transformed into a sly grin. "Don't worry, Bradford. That was the easiest one. Don't expect to get anymore right," Mallard sneered.

"Okay, bring it on," Bradford replied.

"I'd grab a hold of all I can, relentless in my spree, amidst the crimes I hung a man, and then the man hung me. I met some more of my own kind. We really got along in open hide where none could find except the dead and gone," Mallard stated valiantly, a.k.a. courageously, believing Bradford couldn't possibly solve the riddle.

"I'd grab a hold of all I can..." Bradford mumbled. "What could that be? Maybe a handcuff, a snare, or some type of predatory animal? Relentless in my spree... that again could be a snare, considering it catches animals, but it could also be a perilous, a.k.a. treacherous, predator. Amidst the crimes, I hung a man. Again, it could be a noose, but it could also be a metaphor for a snare or predator, trapping an animal or person," Bradford mumbled under his breath.

"Are you hanging in there?" Mallard catechized, meaning interrogated, Bradford, with a wicked grin splattered across his face.

*"Hanging... noose! Hanging and noose, you hang someone with a noose! That's why he mentioned, are you hanging in there?"*

Bradford glanced over towards Mallard, who

was performing his victory dance, move it out and shake it out, take it back and shake it out, step left and slide, step right and slide.

*Why is he dancing when his riddle just got cracked? Unless he's trying to fool me....* Bradford thought. "May I have more time?" he asked.

Mallard's grin diminished into an angry scowl. "You smart meager rascal, you won't get the answer anyways. Go on with your miserable thinking."

"Thank you," Bradford replied, grateful and filled with gratitude that he was still breathing.

*Then the man hung me. It can't be a predator because the dead man could not kill the predator. It has to be some sort of trap!* Bradford thought.

"Time's running out, Bradford!" Mallard said.

"There's no time limit!" he retorted back.

"My rules!" Mallard shouted back. "Fifteen seconds, you better get to thinking."

Bradford looked around the room, and that was when he saw a spider web. *Could that be it? Hung a man, yeah, that could be a web. Then the man hung me. That can also be a web, and it grabs ahold of everything it can!*

"5, 4, 3, 2—" Mallard sang.

"I have my answer!" Bradford blurted out.

"Go on..." Mallard replied.

"A spider web, final answer," Bradford stated.

Mallard's face flushed with bewilderment. "This isn't possible! How? How did you get two riddles correct?"

"Honestly, they weren't that hard. You should find a more challenging one, but you won't be able find one that I won't be able to crack. I have an IQ of 468. Take your best shot. Once I win, Malinfesa will demote you and strip you from your immortality status," Bradford said.

Although Bradford was confident, he was attempting to get under Mallard's skin and throw him off his game, so he wouldn't be able to play any more mind games with Bradford.

"Give me your final riddle, and we can put this whole thing to bed, sooner than later," Bradford said.

"If you insist," Mallard said as blood drained from his semitranslucent face. "Who makes it, has no need of it, who buys it, has no use for it, who uses it, can neither see nor feel it. What is it?" Mallard stated.

*What could this be? Who makes it, has no need of it. Maybe someone manufactured some sort of a product, they don't use themselves? 'Who buys it, has no use for it. Maybe a gift, wrapping paper? Maybe a test or worksheets because teachers have no use for materials kids use? Neither of those really makes sense, though. Who uses it, can neither see nor feel it. No idea?* Branford thought.

"I can't solve this. You might as well throw me in my coffin right now," Bradford said, a defeated tinge in his voice.

This wasn't the end of Bradford. He noticed on the word "coffin" Mallard flinched as if it meant something important to him. Before Mallard could respond, Bradford yelled, "I take it back. I don't give up!"

*Okay, coffin. How could a coffin be important? Maybe Mallard was scared he was going to get thrown in his. Let's try a coffin. Maybe it could solve the riddle.* Bradford thought filled with ambiguity, a word, which also means doubt. *Who makes it, has no use for it. That works with a coffin, but it works with almost all items manufactured by mankind. Who buys it, has no use for it. Most people don't buy their own coffins, so I guess that works. Who uses it, can neither see nor feel it. You can't feel or see a coffin if you're dead so yeah, that works. That could be it, so I might as well roll the dice. It's not like I have any other brilliant ideas.*

"A coffin, final answer" Bradford stated. While waiting to find out his fate, his stomach dropped as if he was riding a roller coaster headed 90 degrees downward at 500 mph.

Mallard didn't respond, but an open door appeared behind Bradford. He was about to bolt out until Mallard started to mumble.

"Prophecy?" Mallard announced in defeat as his body began to disintegrate, and his voice echoed more and more.

*" 'To be or not to be, that is the question.'*
**The final act is upon us.**
*'All the world's a stage and all the men and women are merely players.'*
**The Power Inside is powerless.**

*'Some are born great, some achieve greatness, and some have greatness thrust upon them.'*
**Unless The Power is destroyed, The Power Inside will wither away forever.**
*'Nothing will come from nothing.'*
**The Power Slayer is hidden in plain sight.**
*'Now is the winter of our discontent.'*
**Possess it and master it, and there will be warmth."**

Bradford engraved every word in his mind, including the Shakespearian quotes, and then ran out backwards out of that godforsaken macabre, a word which means frightening place, as swiftly as he could.

# CHAPTER 8: APPARENTLY, I'M A HEINOUS KILLER...WHAT?

Bradford cannonballed backward into the hallway. His friends were anxiously awaiting his arrival. As he magically reappeared after walking through a solid wall, they had no idea where he had vanished and how he had reappeared. Apparently, only Bradford could enter through the Health Office door. Everyone else just saw and felt a solid wall. There was no way for anyone else to follow Bradford into Mallard's SECRET bunker with the daunting WEB Mallard spun that almost put Bradford in a COFFIN. Bradford hurriedly explained everything that had transpired with Mallard.

"There is no time to dillydally, we must decode the prophecy. The first two lines are "'To be or not to be, that is the question'. The final act is upon us," Bradford stated.

"That's easy. We are close to the end, and we may die soon. So what's new?" Andy asked.

Everyone agreed, and Bradford moved on to

the third and fourth verse.

"'All the world's a stage and all the men and women are merely players.' The Power Inside is powerless," Bradford continued.

"I got this! It means we all play a role, and Bradford is 'The Power Inside,'" A.K. said.

A.K. then explained the incident at the mall when the squirrels were trying to take Bradford's power inside from him, in order to save his life.

"Wow, and I just thought you squirrels in the mall were possessed. I wonder how things would have turned out if I had relinquished my powers to you back then. Wait, why can't I relinquish my power to you now?" Bradford inquired.

"It doesn't work like that, my friend. Unfortunately, only Mother Nature could have helped us, and now the time window has lapsed. We failed you and the mission at the mall." A.K. gloomy answered.

"Okay, we can't ponder on what could have been. We must concentrate. The third and fourth verses mean we all play a role, and I have no power. Great, what's new?" Bradford yelled, with his rage knowing no end.

Suddenly, Bradford's anger transmuted into sheer panic as a stampede of footsteps were approaching closer and closer. Bradford couldn't believe his eyes. It was Mr. Abram, Spike, and the 399 heroic squirrels, who had rescued Bradford and his friends in the Detention room. Everyone's mouth dropped.

"How could this be? After the curse had left

Mr. Abram's body, he had fallen to his death," Bradford gushed in amazement.

"The squirrels' sudden departure from the Detention room was due to them making a squirrel rope by interlocking paws and saving me in the nick of time. Then as we were about to flee, I noticed the other teachers still under the curse of Malinfesa turned on Spike, and they were about to shish kebab him. The squirrels and I rescued Spike and got away, just in the nick of time," Mr. Abram explained.

Spike pleaded for forgiveness. Bradford was not sure if he could ever trust Spike again, but what could he do at this time? They were running out of time, and he wasn't sure if Spike could do any more harm than already inflicted. Bradford brought Mr. Abram and Spike up to speed on all that had transpired.

"Now let's move on and see if we can decode any more. The fifth and sixth phrases are, 'Some are born great, some achieve greatness, and some have greatness thrust upon them.' Unless The Power is destroyed, The Power Inside will wither away forever," Bradford stated.

"That's easy!" Mr. Abram declared. "The Power is Malinfesa. That's what we always address the curse by, 'The Power'."

Bradford's eyes bulged, and he bawled, "Unless I rise to the occasion and defeat Malinfesa, I will die at the age of 14."

Although Bradford had near death experiences in the past day, dying had never crossed his mind. This time, it was different, and the reality had set in as it was clearly stated in the prophecy. He must defeat Malinfesa or else die.

As Bradford froze in his track, as if a pack of wolves had surrounded him, Maverick took control of the conversation. "Okay, so far, we have decoded that time is running out, and unless we find how to defeat Malinfesa, Bradford will die. Let's move forward. Bradford, snap out of it. What's after the sixth phrase?" Maverick asked.

Before having any more processing time, Bradford's thoughts were cut short by the school bell starting a new school day. In confusion, he noticed he was no longer in the endless twilight zone hall. He was now standing in front of the school with all the other students, his friends and Mr. Abram standing next to him. He snapped out of his daze when he heard a scream.

"AAAAAAAH, WHY IS THERE A SQUIRREL STANDING ON MAVERICK'S SHOULDER?"

Bradford chuckled and waited for the school doors to open as he saw all the squirrels with the exception of A.K., disbursing into the school and up the trees.

"All students and teachers, please meet in the library!" Mrs. Bloomer's voice rang through the loudspeaker. "For everyone's safety, we need everyone confined as there could be a heinous killer on our school premises. If you see anyone with a weapon, report them to a teacher with a 'Stay Safe' pin immediately, and we will handle it from there."

This was followed by students' protests, cries, and screeches all the way to the library.

"A little bit overdramatic. Don't they know it's only a bunch of possessed demonic teachers trying to capture and kill me? Oh, right, they don't know that," Bradford mumbled.

As everyone walked through the halls, it seemed like a normal day except for the fact that everyone was watching their backs. Some students isolated themselves and spaced out from others as to minimize their odds of being slaughtered. Other students banded together in the hopes of capturing the killer and notifying the teachers. Bradford was one of the coadjutors, but it wasn't for the same reason as the other unsuspecting and naive students. Bradford joined forces with his friends to try and further decode the prophecy. Once in the library, Bradford and the gang occupied a table in the far right corner of the library, hidden away from all the commotion.

"Time is ticking. We must keep decoding the prophecy. The seventh and eight phrases are, 'Nothing will come from nothing.' The Power Slayer is hidden in plain sight," Bradford said.

"The Power Slayer is the sword. I was promised that the sword would be mine to add to my sword collection if Malinfesa defeated Bradford," Spike confessed sheepishly.

Bradford clenched his teeth and took a deep breath to prevent himself from strangling Spike. Bradford thought, *His name is befitting. He has lots of thorns and will prick you when given the opportunity.*

"We must assert ourselves to find the sword that's somewhere right under our nose," Spike uttered while being shamefaced.

Bradford couldn't contain himself any longer. "Really? Do you want to find the sword to defeat Malinfesa or to add it to your despicable sword collection?" Bradford gritted his teeth and spewed in a whisper, so he didn't draw too much attention to them.

"Bradford, I know you're peeved with Spike's betrayal. We all are. However, right now, time isn't on our side. If Malinfesa strikes without us finding the sword, we'll have no chance of defeating it," Miranda voiced softly and lovingly. "Everyone deserves a second chance, right?" Miranda leaned over and gingerly placed her hand on Bradford's shoulder.

Bradford felt a surge of warmth and tranquility throughout his body. "You're right, Miranda. It's water under the bridge. The final two phases are, 'Now is the Winter of our discontent.' Possess it and master it, and there will be warmth."

Bradford remembered reading this ninth phrase in Shakespeare's *Richard III*.

"If we find the sword and I learn how to use it to destroy Malinfesa, we'll all survive," Bradford triumphantly declared.

"Okay, but how are we supposed to find the sword?" Miranda asked.

"Well, we're stuck here in the library anyway,

so we might as well do some research. It's not like there's going to be a sword laying around in the library. We may find some important information about curses and how to use the sword and defeat the curse," Bradford replied.

"Bradford's right. It's not like there will be a sword displayed here in the library. Let's read and learn as much as we can about this curse," Maverick said.

The rest of the group nodded in agreement.

"Let's break up into groups of two," Spike suggested. "These demons could be anywhere, and we can't risk dying."

"Let's make quick groups then," Bradford said. "Maverick and Miranda, A.K. and Andy, Mr. Abram and Spike."

"There's still you," Andy stated.

"I'll be fine by myself," Bradford replied. "I'm going to somehow slash a curse, which has taken the souls of some of the smartest people in history. I can manage surviving in a library filled with people. The teachers wouldn't dare kill me in front of the entire school."

"Whatever you say," Andy responded. "You're right we're just going to roam around the library and read books that may help us defeat Malinfesa."

"Exactly!" Bradford responded. "Now disperse. We better get to work. Otherwise, the day will slip right through our hands."

Bradford watched as his friends moved in different directions, all of them trying their hardest to help him. They genuinely cared about him, and he had never felt so much love and affection in his entire life from his friends.

    *They're putting their lives at stake for me, but why?* he thought. Nevertheless, he was very appreciative and grateful that they cared so much.

# CHAPTER 9: GEM OF DEAD MEN

*W*here should I start? Maybe in the autobiography section, perhaps some genius documented information about a demon curse. *Dang, I sound stupid. Ay! Off-track...keep thinking. Okay, off to the autobiography section. The author must be over 100 years old as the curse surfaces and kills victims every century. I'll start with an extraordinary writer,* Bradford thought.

His eyes were magnetically drawn to the autobiography of Thomas Jefferson. *Being extremely bright, a seasoned writer, and the third President of the United States, he may have written something useful that may help me,* Bradford thought.

Bradford grabbed the book and started power reading. Less than a minute later, on page 27, he came across some underlined sentences. *"Thou may be intelligent, but that does not mean thou should wield a sword. Rather, thou should use thy intelligence to thy advantage. At times, entrapment in lieu of dueling, may be the best course of action."*

Bradford reread the passage and swore that Thomas Jefferson was trying to tell him something, peering through Bradford's soul as if he possessed the key Bradford was so desperately seeking. As Bradford was trying to decode the underlined sentences, he felt a force surge through his body. That was when he was certain the passage, although written hundreds of years ago, was indeed directed at him. He had to learn more.

*"Furthermore, certain missions are best executed in isolation! Don't confide in anyone, especially your Fidus Achates. As others may deceive or hinder, thou and make thou drown in thy own blood, until there is no more of, thou,"* read the next lines.

*Well, that's dark,* Bradford thought. *Fidus Achates is a faithful friend or devoted follower. I guess I'm not telling my friends. The outcome doesn't sound pleasant.*

After twelve more pages, more sentences were underlined. *"I once encountered a Native American tribe. They performed rituals shaking spears, up and up and up. They then initiated a search to find three astute men and located their priceless gems. Once they collected all three gems, they assembled 'The Power Slayer' in the attempts to defeat 'The Power',"* the book stated.

*The Power Slayer in the attempt to defeat The Power,* Bradford thought. *This must be how I can destroy the curse of Malinfesa! From the prophecy, I know The Power Slayer is the sword and The Power is Malinfesa. To acquire the sword, I first need to find the gems. Now where do I start? I'm guessing one of the three individuals possessing the gems is Thomas Jefferson, con-*

*sidering he was a genius and knew about the curse, but how can I find a gem of a dead man? One must be me. Otherwise, why would Malinfesa target me, but who could the third person be? And was Jefferson referring to a metaphorical or physical gem?*

Bradford kept on reading in search of more information, but there was nothing. He reread the third underlined passage and scrutinized the words carefully. *Why did he say the Native Americans were shaking spears? I've read numerous books on Native Americans' rituals, and there was nothing about shaking spears or collecting astute peoples' gems. He must be metaphorically referring to shaking spears as someone or something, and combining their gems and creating a sword, which could slash Malinfesa,* Bradford thought.

Bradford then glanced up at Thomas Jefferson's portrait hanging high on the library wall in admiration and whispered, "Thank you." Bradford wasn't sure if his mind was playing tricks on him, but he could have sworn that Jefferson's portrait's eyes followed him and cracked a slight smile just like Mona Lisa's mischievous smile and piercing roaming eyes are famous for.

While admiring Jefferson's portrait, one of the best writers of all time, Bradford caught sight of a small red shiny glint at the bottom left corner of Jefferson's portrait. Bradford noticed it was the glistening glint of a ruby gem. Why was there a gem hidden behind Jefferson's portrait? As Bradford approached the painting, he heard a blaring noise from the loudspeaker.

"All students, pay close attention please! Will everyone look around? If you spot Bradford Flack, the 14-year-old child prodigy, please make sure to detain him and bring him to the front of the library," The loud voice boomed.

Bradford felt the heat of several football players staring right at him with laser beam eyes. In the nick of time, Bradford leaped up high towards Jefferson's portrait and with the tip of his right index finger, managed to fling the portrait across the room. He caught the ruby gem midair and frantically stuffed it in his pocket as he hit the floor. He felt the grubby hands of people and was carried away to the front of the library. The teachers smiled and signaled for the kids to bring Bradford over to them. They were signaling, "We'll take care of him now." Mrs. Bloomer had a firm grip on his shoulder and wasn't about to let go. As they walked out of the library and down the main hall, Bradford felt Mrs. Bloomer's grip loosen. As he turned around, he saw Spike standing behind him with a one of a kind retractable pocket sword.

"The sword collection comes in handy," Spike announced bashfully.

He didn't stab her. I know we all wanted him to stab her, but he just knocked her out with the hilt of his sword.

"We'll take care of the rest. Continue your research," Maverick stated from behind Spike.

All his other friends and Mr. Abram nodded

in agreement. Bradford gave them a slight head nod and bolted back towards the Thomas Jefferson section. In his rush to get more information, he kept thinking of the shaking spears line. *Why would Thomas Jefferson add that sentence when it's factually incorrect? Native Americans never shook their spears in rituals.* Bradford didn't know what to make of this phrase until he spotted the portrait, which used to be adjacent to Jefferson's portrait. Bradford thought, *It was Shakespeare, shake-speare, shaking spears. Thomas Jefferson must have been referring to Shakespeare!* Bradford couldn't believe that he didn't decode this earlier being every other line of the prophecy was a quote from Shakespeare. He saw the same sparkly glint, which was under Jefferson's painting. Bradford took a quick glance behind him and realized that the jocks were encroaching in on him. He swiftly removed the painting and was awaited by a gleaming forest green emerald. Bradford snatched it up and noticed he was cornered. The kids were closing in on him from all directions, and he was backing up with every step they took forward. This ended when Bradford felt his feet fly out from underneath him as he spiraled downward into a black abyss.

He felt the cold hard floor by the sound of his rear end slamming against the concrete floor. He looked up, and to his surprise, he had landed right beneath his school locker. Bradford got up and hastily opened it. The locker consisted of mostly textbooks and school-related material, but there was one item, which wasn't school-related. It was the small pouch his father had given him a couple of days prior to his passing.

Bradford remembered when his father placed the pouch in his hand and stated the words, "This is an heirloom from your distant relative Albert Einstein. Only open the pouch when in dire need. Otherwise, it will come back and bite you on the backside." Bradford cracked a smile as the thought of that memory made him feel close to his father's presence.

He thought, *My backside hurts enough. It wouldn't be too terrible if I got bit there. Besides, this may be my only chance to see what's inside.*

Bradford's hands were trembling. He had been waiting to open this pouch ever since his dad had given it to him, and the moment had finally arrived. Before he revealed what was inside the pouch, he thought about everything that had transpired because of this curse. He had recently met some of his closest friends. He felt the sensation of being needed, cared for, and a sense of belonging and purpose from kids around the same age as him. He had made friends with courageous and loyal talking squirrels. If anything, this curse may have enhanced Bradford's social life. And with a slight hesitation, Bradford slowly started to open the pouch. His entire body was quivering. The pouch started to unravel, and Bradford shut his eyes. He felt what was inside and fitted it in his right palm. He slowly peeked through his scrunched-up eyes and was greeted by a gorgeous royal blue sapphire.

Bradford grinned at the beautiful, sparkly, exuberant gem and looked away from his locker. He then directed his eyes towards the sky and announced, "Thanks, Dad!"

He could have sworn the cloud he was gazing at winked at him. He then noticed the cloud's face contorted into an angry expression. Bradford admired the gem for a split second more and then grasped it in the palm of his still shaking hand. The second his hand and the gem reconnected, he was piloted into a new dimension.

Bradford saw the image of his father in a room. The room looked very familiar as if Bradford had been there before.

"Dad! Dad!" Bradford shouted as he ran to embrace his father.

When Bradford tried to embrace his dad, he noticed his body went right through his dad's body. This must be an illusion. Bradford inspected the room meticulously and saw a translucent image across from his father. It was Mallard! Bradford then heard the riddle he was asked right before he escaped. "Who makes it, has no need of it, who buys it, has no use for it, who uses it can neither see nor feel it. What is it?" Mallard had asked.

Bradford saw distress flood over his father's face. He couldn't fail! He had to pass. It was his dad. Bradford then heard the voice of Mallard counting down from 10. Bradford watched carefully, his heart thumping in terror as his dad was frozen.

"I-I'm not sure," Bradford's dad announced in complete defeat.

"Five, four, three, two, one," Mallard said, a grin spreading across his face. "Seems like you're out of time… you know what that means!"

Bradford watched in horror as Mallard contorted his hands as if he were extracting something with a look of gratification beaming from his wicked face. Bradford then noticed something was being extracted from his father's body. It was a dark blue silhouette, which was being defiantly hauled out of his dad's body. Bradford realized this must be the soul of a person.

"DADDY!" Bradford cried out, "NO! DON'T DO THIS!"

Mallard shrugged without acknowledging Bradford and said, "That was exhilarating. He's gone now."

Bradford was livid, his body boiling as if he was sunbathing with cooking oil inches away from the sun. He started to shed uncontrollable tears. Bradford barely ever cried, but he couldn't hold back the tsunami of tears that ensued. He felt as if he had been stabbed by the sharpest and most painful sword ever. His father was taken by someone he had defeated. He was now glad that he had destroyed Mallard. He deciphered that his father had shown him this image to enrage and empower him to defeat Malinfesa. At that moment, Bradford made an oath, that his dad will not die in vain. Bradford then collected himself and pushed away the nightmarish images he had just witnessed. He was now back at his locker where he saw the cloud. He knew his father was watching over him.

"This is for you, Dad." Bradford announced, paled face and expressionless, as if he were stone cold, not allowing anyone or anything from standing in his way of defeating Malinfesa.

Bradford, as if possessed with immeasurable force, placed all three gems in his grasp and barreled them to the floor. He kept a weathered eye on the gems as they shattered into tiny shards. Bradford stared, mesmerized at the shards adorning the unyielding earth as if he were in a trance. After a few minutes of leering at the broken shards, Bradford snapped back into reality. What did he just do? He scooped up pieces of the shards from the gems and in desperation started assembling them hoping something good would transpire. Bradford stationed the blue gem in the middle of the three, the green on the right, and lastly, the red on the left. He watched in awe as he saw the three gems spiral in a miniature tornado and transformed into a spectacular, shiny, gleaming, multi-color, embellished sword.

Bradford stared at the sword. It was beautiful! He started to swish it around because it was light for a sword made of minerals. Bradford remembered his childhood when he and his father used to fence with each other and shed a tear, merely thinking about it. He quickly cycled through the lessons his father had taught him as a child, like how to parry and how to jab. Bradford went over the moves, and the sword felt so natural in his hands as if it was his pencil writing down his test answers. He felt like nothing could go wrong when he had possession of the sword. Bradford then remembered Thomas Jefferson's verse. *"entrapment in lieu of dueling."* He must trap the curse, not fight it. He knew the sword would be a key component in destroying the curse but not the main integrant. He had to think of a plan to lure, draw out, and entrap Malinfesa!

Lost in his thoughts, Bradford didn't notice the approaching footsteps. He felt a warm hand graze across his right shoulder. He spun around, and to his surprise, it was his mom with her usual warm and loving smile. Bradford thought, *She's not due back from her business trip for another two days.*

"Mom? Why are you here?" Bradford asked, confused.

"I have been watching your every move," His mom replied, a guilty look across her face.

"What? Why?" Bradford retorted. "You're supposed to be on a work trip, and why are you stalking me?"

"After your father's passing, I wanted to make sure you were safe," Bradford's mom said, looking down at the ground. "I came out from hiding because I wanted to help you conjure up a plan to destroy Malinfesa."

"Go on," Bradford responded.

"As you know, the curse possesses much

more power than you or any human being." Bradford's mother said.

Bradford nodded his head in agreement.

"You also know that the curse has possessed and abducted people you respect and care for and used them to its advantage to lure you into its traps," his mom continued.

Bradford thought about it for a second, and she was right. He nodded again as he thought of his teachers being possessed, and his friends being entrapped in the Detention room and how he barely made it out of the Health Office. There was also no denying the prophecy. He had to save all his loved ones and the World from the wrath of Malinfesa.

Bradford was jolted from his thoughts as his mom adamantly declared, "I believe we should set up a trap and present me as bait. When Malinfesa surfaces, you can slash it away, and we will all live happily ever after."

"That's a great idea!" Bradford complemented. "We better hurry. Otherwise, we'll lose the element of surprise, and we won't be able to perform the plan. What can be the trap?"

His mom's eyes lit up. "Oh, I have one!"

Bradford noticed her eyes. They had literally lit up, and they were purple. Then he noticed a purple figure, with devilishly piercing red eyes, escaping through his mom's mouth. Bradford realized it must be the curse of Malinfesa.

"Oh, god, my mom is possessed." Bradford bolted the other direction and took a right. In desperation, he scurried into the first room he saw —the Health Office. He didn't know what to do because he was cornered. Bradford challenged the purple figure lingering behind him to solve a riddle. Mallard's chair sat empty, so Bradford gravitated towards the chair and sat down without hesitation and stared at the purple figure, mesmerized.

"Hurry up and ask a riddle. I don't have all day. Actually, I do. I have until eternity." A raspy voice echoed, from the purple figure, sending shivers down Bradford's spine.

He was now able to ask a riddle. Malinfesa's power was in his hands. If Malinfesa could not answer the riddle, he would live, and if Malinfesa solved the riddle, Bradford and potentially all mankind would perish.

Bradford's breath was rapid, his heartbeat was accelerated, and his hands were quivering.

"Here goes nothing..." Bradford muttered.

Bradford wasn't a big riddle guy. As he frantically racked his brain, he knew he had to think of one quickly. He thought really hard, and he remembered one from when he was just ten. He remembered his father asking him this riddle. Bradford knew this riddle could be the one to defeat Malinfesa. He was willing to bet his life on it!

As his voice cracked, Bradford unleashed his riddle. "I speak without a mouth and hear without ears. I have no body, but I come alive with wind. What am I?"

Bradford stared through Malinfesa's vile red

eyes and evil purple soul, praying that he would be able to defeat this curse. Bradford noticed Malinfesa's eyes perk up as if she knew the answer to the riddle and the curse then followed that up with a sly grin as if she was positive she knew the correct answer. Bradford felt a spike of fear course through his veins. Is this the end of Bradford, or is it the end of Malinfesa?

Bradford watched as Malinfesa started to respond with an answer.

"A river," Malinfesa calmly stated.

Bradford was in shock. He will survive!

"Incorrect, the correct answer is an echo," Bradford announced with triumph in his voice.

Malinfesa's eyes turned from a dark red to a bright red, and they were swarming with heat as if she were about to explode. The creature lunged at Bradford, but before she could reach him, Malinfesa's soul flew out from her body. The purple figure fell to the ground lifeless. Bradford saw the spirit of the curse. It was so defenseless. Bradford knew what he had to do, so he grabbed his sword, which was resting beside him and then took his shot.

Bradford slashed away the last remains of the curse of Malinfesa, saving himself and mankind from eternal destruction.

Bradford picked up his sword, looked upward, and announced, "This was for you, Dad. Thank you!"

# CHAPTER 10: WAS IT ALL A DREAM?

After Bradford's encounter with Malinfesa, I have spent much time investigating Bradford's life and beyond. To my knowledge, there has never been another genius to be targeted and/or harmed by Malinfesa. I'm not sure whether Malinfesa was too weak to fight another foe or if she still lies dead in Mallard's bunker with all the countless dead bodies. All I know is that when Bradford exited Mallard's bunker once and for all, his life only became stranger.

Bradford strolled into the library with a feeling of pride and redemption, he had defeated the curse of Malinfesa once and for all, at least from his assessment. But as he strolled into the library, he was greeted by just the librarian.

*Where is everyone?* Bradford thought as he scratched his head.

"Hi, Bradford, shouldn't you be in class?" Ms. Deja Vu, the librarian, asked.

Bradford looked around puzzled and glanced at the clock. It was 9:17 a.m. Second period had already started. Bradford then leaned forward and spotted Thomas Jefferson's and Shakespeare's portraits, and it seems as if they were never touched, let alone flung across the library. It was as if nothing ever happened.

"Yeah, I should get to class," Bradford responded.

As he left the library, he was greeted by a familiar figure.

"A.K., I'm so glad to see you! I have so much to tell you!" Bradford said.

A.K. tilted his head and started to slowly back up.

"A.K., It's me!" Bradford exclaimed.

"Are you talking to a squirrel?" A puzzled voice asked from behind him.

Bradford whipped around, and his face started to flush.

"Umm, yeah, it's A.K. Do you not remember him, Miranda?" Bradford stuttered.

Miranda laughed. "He's a squirrel, and how do you know my name?"

"Do you not remember me? I'm Bradford," he said.

"I don't think we've met before," Miranda replied.

"Well, I have to go to class," Bradford said, scurrying off.

"It was nice meeting you, Bradford! Maybe I'll see you around!" Miranda shouted.

"Yeah, see you around," he responded, without turning around.

Miranda then walked off to wherever her destination was. Bradford headed in the opposite direction towards his Spanish class.

"Hola, Bradford, Donde has estado?" Mrs. Ramirez inquired.

"Sorry, I got a bit distracted," he replied.

Bradford scooted into his seat right in front of Mrs. Ramirez. What if she was still possessed? Throughout the entire class, Bradford watched Mrs. Ramirez closely; seeing if there were any signs that she may still be possessed. As time passed, Bradford found no signs. The bell rang, and Bradford found himself strolling out of Spanish class without being chased by a demon.

He spotted Andy before entering third period and approached him briskly.

"Andy! Remember Spike, Maverick, Miranda, and the curse?" Bradford asked.

"What are you talking about? Who are these people, and what curse?" Andy asked in confusion.

"Never mind," Bradford responded, shaking his head.

When Bradford scurried into Ms. Maegan's AP English class, he was expecting her to devour everyone up alive, but she acted civilized, ironically teaching them about Shakespeare.

In fourth period AP Physics, he spotted Dorothy. Was that her or a clone as Mallard had claimed? Mrs. Bloomer was also in class, ready to teach as if nothing had ever happened. *But she was knocked unconscious with the hilt of Spike's sword. How can this be?* Bradford thought.

During lunch Miranda approached Bradford and introduced him to Spike and Maverick as if they were meeting for the first time. Even the outdoor courtyard seemed to be buzzing with kids during lunch.

In Ms. Mowie's fifth period AP History class, nothing out of the ordinary occurred except that it was ordinary. It was as if everyone had forgotten about what had happened.

In sixth period, Mr. Abram acted like his old chipper self, and Derrick was sitting next to him. Again, was that Derrick or a clone?

Now that Malinfesa was defeated, Bradford had more questions than answers.

When he arrived home, Bradford's mom was waiting for him with a souvenir from her business trip and his favorite pasta dish. It was a good thing she had prepared food as Bradford was starving from his two-day involuntary fast. His mom claimed she returned home early from her business trip as her client had a family emergency.

*Didn't she remember she came to school and confessed that she knew about Malinfesa and tried to devise a plan to destroy the curse, only to become possessed by it?* Bradford thought.

When he unwrapped the souvenir his mom had bought for him, he was holding the Power Slayer, the multicolor gem sword that Bradford serendipitously created from smashing the three ancient gemstones used to destroy Malinfesa. Given his day at school was so bizarre, it never dawned on him that he didn't have the sword in his possession upon returning to the library and throughout the school day.

That next morning as Bradford was putting on his shoes to go to school, he felt a searing pain in his left hand and noticed a small puncture hole on the face of his right shoe, the same hole that Mr. Abram had punctured through his shoe while trying to devour A.K. Was the hole in his shoe a puncture mark or a hole from wear and tear? He couldn't explain the searing pain in his left hand until he remembered injuring it at the mall before he mysteriously ended up in Mr. Abram's calculus class.

In the months to follow, strange things continued as if nothing had ever happened. One good thing was that Bradford did, in fact, become friends with Maverick and Spike, and he and Miranda started dating. Even the jocks stopped bullying him in the outdoor courtyard.

In his senior year, Bradford was accepted to Harvard at the age of 15, and he was officially entered into *The Guinness World Records* as the smartest person to ever live.

I had previously advised you to close this book. In doing so, you can think Bradford easily destroyed the curse, saving everyone. If you are still reading, then you may witness catastrophe firsthand. Now that you have read the book, do you think there was a "happily ever after" with Bradford slashing the curse away and saving the world, or do you think there is more than meets the eye with catastrophic ramifications?

# ABOUT THE AUTHOR

## Shaya Dadmehr

 Shaya Dadmehr is proud to share "Detention" with you. This is his second published book, the first being "Greek Gods for Kids". Shaya is an outgoing, witty, curious, and at times sarcastic 11-year-old boy. Shaya thoroughly enjoys sports such as basketball, football and martial arts and has the travel bug for new destinations, so he can learn and experience various cultures and lifestyles. Shaya has a fondness for reading, writing, history, and arithmetic. Shaya's favorite topics to write about are personal narratives, current events, fantasy, and mythology. When writing, Shaya's advice is, "if you get writer's block, take a break, go do something new, fun and/or relaxing and when an idea pops into your head, race toward your computer, or piece of paper, and write feverishly." Most importantly, his advice is to read an array of books and articles whenever time allows; for when you read, it opens your mind and imagination to new

and exciting events and worlds; undoubtedly, making you a better author and a more interesting person, as a whole.

Thank you for reading my book :)
-Shaya Dadmehr